W9-AOQ-213

Dora's Book

Dora's Book

by Michelle Edwards

Carolrhoda Books, Inc./Minneapolis

c. 1

Library of Congress Cataloging-in-Publication Data

Edwards, Michelle.
    Dora's book / story and illustrations by Michelle Edwards.
        p.   cm.
    Summary: Having written and illustrated a book about her
grandparents, Dora asks her friend Tom for help in printing and
binding it.
    ISBN 0-87614-441-3 (lib. bdg.)
    [1. Books—Fiction. 2. Printing—Fiction.] I. Title.
PZ7.E262Do   1990
[E]—dc20   89-71244
                                                        CIP
                                                        AC

Manufactured in the United States of America

1 2 3 4 5 6 7 8 9 10 99 98 97 96 95 94 93 92 91 90

*In memory of Valerie Leavis,
a good friend and neighbor*

In northern Minnesota, where the winters are
fierce, there lived an old woman named Dora.
When the days grew short and the winds blew cold,
Dora stayed inside, trying to keep warm. Snug and
toasty under her favorite quilt, Dora liked to think
about her Grandma Molly and her Grandpa Max.

One night after dinner, Dora decided that before she got any older or any more forgetful, she would write down all the things she could remember about Grandma Molly and Grandpa Max and the way they lived a long time ago.

Dora wrote about how Grandpa Max gathered sticks from the oak tree in the front yard and whittled them into knitting needles for Grandma Molly.

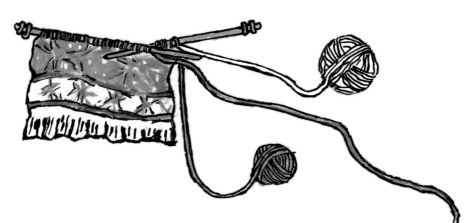

She told how Grandma Molly used to sit in her special chair, knitting and purling sweaters, hats, and mittens for everyone she knew.

She told how Grandma Molly rolled out dough as thin as paper for her strudel,

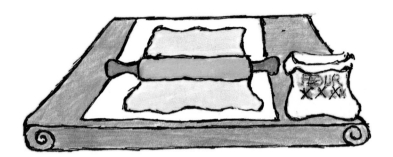

and how Grandpa Max sawed and hammered wood to make their furniture.

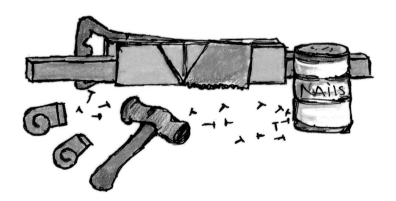

All winter long, Dora wrote and wrote and wrote. She worked hard to make sure that the words told exactly what she remembered. But there were some things, like Grandma Molly's smile and Grandpa Max's long beard, that needed pictures.

In the spring, Dora took out her pencils and began to draw. She drew and erased and drew and erased. She drew pictures of Molly and Max.

She drew their house in winter, with the snow piled
high, and their garden in summer, full of tomatoes
and grapes.

She drew their parlor, with the reading chair
Grandpa Max had made and the rug Grandma Molly
had braided. And she drew their kitchen, with the big
old black stove.

In the summer, Dora finished drawing. She gathered up her pictures and stories and took them across town to show to her best friend, Tom.

"Tom, I think I have a book here," said Dora.

Tom was a printer. In his basement, he had an old printing press and drawers and drawers full of little pieces of metal with raised letters on the top. He called these pieces of metal "type."

"Think your old press can print my book?" Dora asked.
"You bet," said Tom. "I've printed lots of books on that old press. But first let's send your drawings to a special place in the city. They'll use them to make metal pictures with lines that stick up, just like the letters on the type do. That way I can print your drawings on my press."

When the metal pictures arrived, they looked just like Dora's drawings, except they were backwards!

"Perfect," said Tom. "That's just how they're supposed to look."

Then Tom showed Dora how to set the type.

They took the metal letters out of the drawers one
by one to make the words of Dora's stories.

Letter by letter, word by word, sentence by sentence, they built a page. On some pages, they put one of the metal pictures with the words. And everything on every page was backwards!

"Perfect," said Tom when he saw the first page. "That's just how it's supposed to look."

"Except . . ." said Dora, "Grandma's name was M-O-L-L-Y, not P-O-L-L-Y." It was Dora's job to check each page for mistakes.

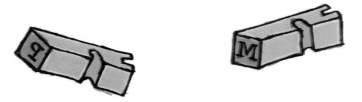

When Tom had fixed all the mistakes, they were ready to print. The book was going to be printed on big sheets of paper with room enough on each sheet for four pages, two on one side and two on the other.

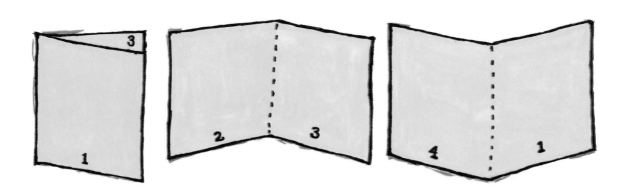

Tom dipped his ink knife into a can of sticky black ink and spread it over the roller on the press.

Clank, clank, clank. Tom turned the handle of the printing press, and the roller rolled over the metal letters and metal pictures. The parts that stuck up were covered with ink. Then the paper and the inky pictures and type were squeezed together. The first page was printed!

When Tom peeled off the paper, it looked just like the metal page, except the pictures and the letters weren't backwards anymore.

Grandpa Max and Grandma Molly lived in a little white house at the end of Oak Street in Hibbing, Minnesota. Grandpa built a picket fence around the house and every spring Grandma painted it.

2

3

"Perfect," said Dora. "Now *that's* just how it's supposed to look."

Page by page, Tom printed all of Dora's pictures
and stories.

Dora helped too. She brought Tom tea and strudel
made from her grandmother's recipe.

When all the pages were printed, there were stacks
and stacks of paper all over Tom's basement.
"And now for the binding." Tom said.

Tom and Dora folded all the pages and put them in
the right order. Then they sewed them together and
glued fancy green paper to the first and last pages.
These were the books' endpapers.

Tom cut pieces of heavy cardboard for the cover and strips of bendy red board for the spine.

Dora cut yards and yards of beautiful green cloth to glue over the cardboard.

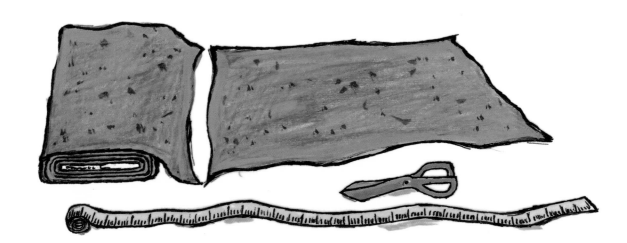

When the covers were done, Tom and Dora glued
them to the endpapers. Then they pressed the books
in the book press. When the glue had dried, the books
were finished.

"Not too bad, Dora," said Tom, handing Dora a book.

"They're beautiful!" exclaimed Dora.
"Got a lot of books there, Dora," said Tom. "Any idea what you'll do with all those books?"

"Have a big party and give them all away, of course," she said. Dora helped Tom sweep the floor and throw away all the little scraps of paper and fabric.

Together they cleaned the type and put it away. Tom cleaned Dora's metal pictures and carefully wrapped them up so she could save them. Then Tom and Dora loaded the books into Dora's red wagon, and Dora took them home.

The next day, Dora baked a big apple strudel and made gallons and gallons of tea in her shiny copper samovar. She invited all of her friends and neighbors to come to her party.

 Tom was guest of honor.

Dora gave everyone a book. In each book, she wrote
something special.

To my neighbor Mrs. Levey

Grandma did paint their picket fence white every year. Except once, she painted it pink just like mine.

Dora M. Skale
Painter

To my fellow gardener Smithy

Hope you like Grandpa's gardening tips. Grandpa always claimed he had the best mulch this side of the Mississippi.

Dora M. Skale
gardener

To my friend Betty

Here are some of the recipes you asked for and never got. It is the extra cup of sugar in the strawberry preserves that does it.

Dora M. Skale
Baker

After the party was over, there were two books left. Dora kept one for herself and one for Tom. In Tom's book, she wrote:

To Tom,
    A good friend
and a great printer.

        Dora M. Skale
        Author

Before the mid-1800s, all books were printed and bound by hand, just like the book that Tom and Dora made. While some people still make books by hand, most books are now made by complex machines.

Michelle Edwards would like to thank the staff of the Minnesota Center for Book Arts for their technical advice about the art of making a book by hand.